*For the Tigers -*
*Noah, Will, Tim and Antonia*
*~JS and TW*

This edition copyright © 2001
Baby's First Book Club ®
Bristol, PA 19007
Originally published in Great Britain 2001 by
Little Tiger Press, London
An Imprint of Magi Publications
Text © 2001 Julie Sykes
Illustrations © 2001 Tim Warnes
All rights reserved • Printed in Belgium
ISBN 1 58048 172 8

# Wait for me, Little Tiger!

by Julie Sykes

illustrated by Tim Warnes

Little Tiger has lots of friends. They liked to play exciting games. Each time he went out to look for them his little sister would say, "I'm lonely. Can I come with you, Little Tiger?"

And Little Tiger would answer,
"No you can't", Little Sister.
"You're too small."

One day, Little Tiger said, "Can I go out to play?"
Mommy Tiger was very busy, so she told him to take
Little Sister along, too.

"I don't want to!" cried Little Tiger. "She's too small
to play with me." But Mommy Tiger wouldn't change her
mind. "She's not too small, if you lend her a paw now and
then," she said.

Crossly, Little Tiger ran off into the jungle.
"Wait for me!" cried Little Sister,
scampering after him.

Little Tiger took Little Sister to visit Little Bear.
They tried bowling, but Little Sister couldn't
roll the ball straight. She missed the pins, and hit
Little Bear instead.

"*Ouch!*" cried Little Bear, nursing her paw. "Perhaps you should find somewhere safer to play."

Little Tiger thought so, too.

"Wait for me!" cried Little Sister, as he hurried toward the trees.

Very soon Little Tiger came across Little Monkey. They both climbed up trees and swung down vines.

But Little Sister couldn't climb trees. She reached the first branch, then fell and landed on top of Little Monkey.

"*Ouch!*" he squeaked.
Little Tiger sighed. He didn't
want to leave his game with Little
Monkey, but it wasn't safe enough
for Little Sister. He would have to
take her away from the trees.
"Wait for me!" cried Little Sister,
bouncing after him.

Little Tiger went to find Little Leopard. His spotted friend was running in the grass. Little Leopard started a game of tag, but Little Sister didn't look where she was going. She tripped on a stone, hurtled forward, and knocked Little Leopard flat on his face.

"*Ow!*" cried Little Leopard. "That hurt!"

Little Tiger was worried he would have no friends left if Little Sister kept causing accidents.

"Come on," he said. "We'd better go somewhere else."

Little Tiger trotted off to the river, where he found Little Elephant on the bank. Little Sister couldn't wait to learn how to swim.

"It's easy," said Little Tiger, jumping in. "You kick your paws and off you go!"

Little Sister didn't find swimming easy. The water splashed in her eyes and she couldn't see where she was going. Suddenly . . .

SPLASH!

Little Elephant jumped in . . .

. . . and Little Sister swallowed a mouthful of water.

"Help!" she spluttered.

Little Tiger towed her safely to the bank.

"Swimming is too dangerous for you," he said.

"You'd better sit and watch."

"I don't *want* to watch. I want to
play with you," she shouted crossly.
"You're too little to play my
games," said Little Tiger.

Little Tiger jumped back into the water.
It was fun splashing around with Little
Elephant. Soon he forgot all about Little Sister
on the bank. He finally remembered her when
the game was finished. "That was fun,
wasn't it, Little Sister?" he called.
There was no answer.

When Little Tiger jumped out of
the water, the riverbank was empty.
His little sister was gone!

Little Tiger felt awful. He should not have left Little Sister on her own. What if she had fallen into the water and been swept away?

Little Elephant helped him search along the riverbank, but they couldn't see her anywhere.

Little Tiger looked
everywhere. He searched the
plains, but she wasn't there.
He hunted in the trees,
but she wasn't there.

He peered inside Little Bear's cave, but she wasn't there either.

Now Little Tiger was frightened.

Mommy Tiger would be angry that he had lost Little Sister.

Sadly, he ran home to tell her.

He was almost there when . . .

"BOO!"

Little Sister leapt down
at him from the trees.

"See, Little Tiger," she cried.
"I've been practicing and
now I can climb trees, too!"

Little Tiger was so pleased that Little Sister was safe.

He wanted to make it up to her for being unkind.

"I'll help you practice bowling next," he offered.

"And running?" asked Little Sister.

"And running," Little Tiger agreed.

"Good," she said. "And after all that, will you help me learn to swim?"

"Maybe," said Little Tiger. "But for now, Little Sister, it's time I helped you home."